W9-ADL-371

This book belongs to

. . . .

For my mother and father
—Alison

For Rebecca (Baby Ginger)
—Aunty Cathy

tiger tales
an imprint of ME Media, LLC
202 Old Ridgefield Road, Wilton, CT 06897
Published in the United States 2002
Originally published in Great Britain 2001,
by Egmont Books Limited

CIP data is available
ISBN 1-58925-372-8
Printed in UAE

1 3 5 7 9 10 8 6 4 2

I Don't Want to Sleep Alone!

by Alison Ritchie
Illustrated by Cathy Gale

tiger tales

Mommy and Daddy had a **big** bed.
They slept in it together.

Joey had his own little bed.
He hardly slept in it at all.

At bedtime, Joey took a bath,
brushed his teeth,
and listened to **three** stories.

He kissed Mommy good night,
he kissed Daddy good night,
and he fell asleep.

But in the middle of the night, he woke up.

"I'm all alone!" he thought.

"I don't like it!"

So

he climbed out of bed and crept into Mommy and Daddy's room. He crawled under the blanket and snuggled up beside them.

He squiggled and wriggled.

His paws poked into Daddy's back.
His whiskers tickled Mommy's face.

The next morning, Mommy was squashed up against Daddy, and Daddy was hanging off the edge of the bed.

"Joey!" said Mommy.

"You must stay in your **own** bed! There isn't enough room for **everybody** in our bed."

"It's not fair!" said Joey.

"You and Daddy are grown-ups, and you don't sleep **alone**. I'm only little, and I have to be **all by myself**."

That night, Mommy gave Joey his favorite toy, Teddy.

"He'll look after you," she said. Joey hugged Mommy and Daddy good night and cuddled Teddy. Then he fell asleep.

But in the middle of the night, Joey woke up.

He went
into Mommy
and Daddy's
room.
The next morning, Daddy
was angry.
"What happened to Teddy?"
he said.
"Teddy squiggled and wriggled
all night long," said Joey.

That night, Daddy gave Joey his **cuddly bunny**. "Bunny won't budge," he said. "He's a very good bunny!"

Joey fell asleep . . .

but in the middle of the night, he crept into Mommy and Daddy's room.

"Bunny kept **poking me** in the back!" he said.

The next night Mommy said wearily, "How about **Monkey**?"

But in the middle of the night . . .

"Monkey kept **tickling me** in the face."

The night after that, everyone was very tired.
"What about **Elephant** tonight?" said Daddy.

But...

in the middle of the night...

"Elephant was **squishing** me."

The next night everyone went to bed very early. "This is **Donkey,**" said Mommy. "I've had him since I was as little as you. Maybe he can help you sleep."

Joey snuggled down with Donkey.

But in the middle of the night . . .

"Donkey kicked me right out of bed!"

"ALRIGHT!

That's it!" said Daddy.

"You've tried Teddy,
Bunny,
Monkey,
Elephant,
and Donkey," said Mommy.

"We've run out of toys, Joey—
what should we do
NOW?"

"**Nothing**," said Joey with a **big** yawn. "There just isn't room for **everybody** in my bed."

"I want to sleep
ALONE!"

And he slept soundly in his **own** bed
all night long.

Did you enjoy this tiger tales book?

More fun-filled and exciting stories await you!
Look for these paperback titles and more at your local library or bookstore. And have fun reading!

Another Fine Mess
by Tony Bonning; illustrated by Sally Hobson
ISBN 1-58925-356-6

Beware of the Bears
by Alan MacDonald; illustrated by Gwyneth Williamson
ISBN 1-58925-359-0

Dora's Eggs
by Julie Sykes; illustrated by Jane Chapman
ISBN 1-58925-365-5

How to Be a Happy Hippo
by Jonathan Shipton; illustrated by Sally Percy
ISBN 1-58925-357-4

I'll Always Love You
by Paeony Lewis; illustrated by Penny Ives
ISBN 1-58925-360-4

Little Mouse and the Big Red Apple
by A.H. Benjamin; illustrated by Gwyneth Williamson
ISBN 1-58925-358-2

Love Is a Handful of Honey
by Giles Andreae; illustrated by Vanessa Cabban
ISBN 1-58925-353-1

Mr. Wolf's Pancakes
by Jan Fearnley
ISBN 1-58925-354-X

Snarlyhissopus
by Alan MacDonald; illustrated by Louise Voce
ISBN 1-58925-370-1

tiger tales
202 Old Ridgefield Road
Wilton, CT 06897